DIRT BIKE CRAZY

YAMAHA DIRT BIKES

By R. L. Van

Kaleidoscope
Minneapolis, MN

The Quest for Discovery Never Ends

....

This edition is co-published by agreement between
Kaleidoscope and World Book, Inc.

Kaleidoscope Publishing, Inc.
6012 Blue Circle Drive
Minnetonka, MN 55343 U.S.A.

World Book, Inc.
180 North LaSalle St., Suite 900
Chicago IL 60601 U.S.A.

All rights reserved. No part of this book may be reproduced
in any form without written permission from the publishers.

Kaleidoscope ISBNs
978-1-64519-095-0 (library bound)
978-1-64494-156-0 (paperback)
978-1-64519-199-5 (ebook)

World Book ISBN
978-0-7166-4368-5 (library bound)

Library of Congress Control Number
2019939021

Text copyright ©2020 by Kaleidoscope Publishing, Inc.
All-Star Sports, Bigfoot Books, and associated logos are
trademarks and/or registered trademarks of Kaleidoscope
Publishing, Inc.

Printed in the United States of America.

Bigfoot lurks within one of the images in this book. It's up to you to find him!

TABLE OF
CONTENTS

Chapter 1: Blaze of Blue **4**

Chapter 2: From Music to Motocross **10**

Chapter 3: Track and Trail **16**

Chapter 4: Yamaha Champs **22**

Beyond the Book 28

Research Ninja 29

Further Resources 30

Glossary 31

Index 32

Photo Credits 32

About the Author 32

CHAPTER 1

Blaze of Blue

Nate's mom sits in the stands. Dinner is in half an hour. Nate swings his leg over his 2019 Yamaha YZ125. He's taking it out for a practice run. It's new. But he's had one before. Yamaha has been making the YZ125 since 1974. This bike is like Nate's 2017 model. He enjoys riding a bike he trusts. His right foot finds the **kick-starter**. He kicks down hard. The bike starts up.

Nate grasps the **throttle**. It's on the right handlebar. He twists it. This revs the bike. He loves the high whining noise. It's the sound of a **two-stroke** engine. Nate puts on his goggles. He takes off! Dirt from the motocross track goes flying. Riding a two-stroke means shifting gears more often. But the YZ125 has an adjustable **clutch**. Nate set it up to pull easily. He approaches a corner. He shifts gears smoothly.

The YZ125 has had few major changes since 2005, but it's still a top competitor.

The YZ125's engine is powerful. Two-stroke engines create a lot of power for their size. Nate once rode a four-stroke bike. It had a bigger engine. But he gets just as much power on this bike. Two-strokes are usually harder to handle. But this bike is light. Nate doesn't have any trouble. He keeps control.

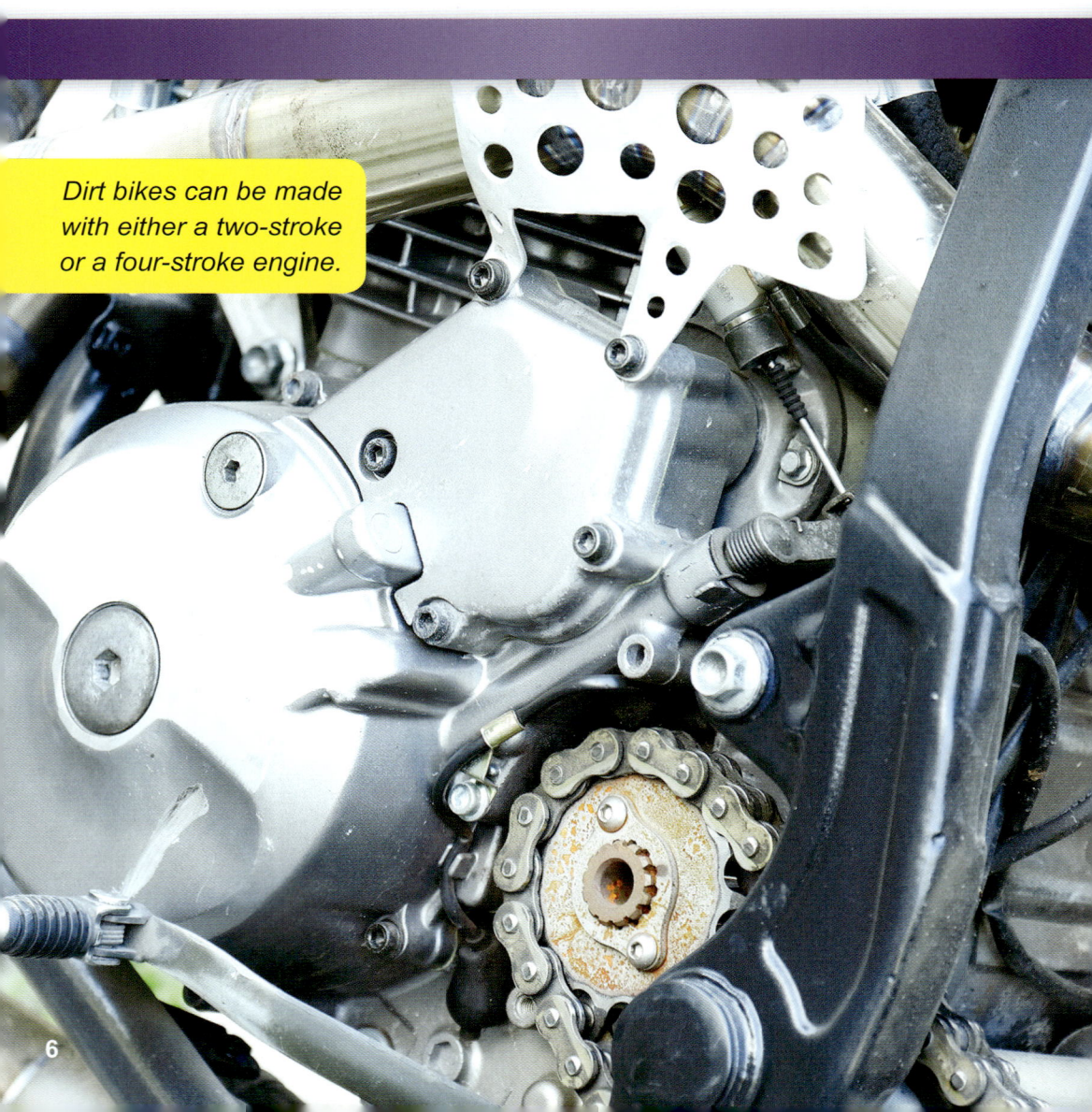

Dirt bikes can be made with either a two-stroke or a four-stroke engine.

Many riders race to success on Yamaha dirt bikes.

The front fender is blue. It seems to bounce as he flies over hills. The bike's **suspension** absorbs the impact. Nate's ride feels smooth. He sees the sun setting on the horizon. He'll need to leave soon. He looks over at his mom. She gives him a thumbs-up. He has time for one more lap. Nate grins. He twists the throttle. He and his YZ125 zoom around the course.

PARTS OF A YAMAHA YZ125

CHAPTER 2

Nippon Gakki's piano frames were useful. The company made motorcycle engine parts with the same strong and flexible metal.

From Music to Motocross

Yamaha wasn't always called Yamaha. And it didn't make dirt bikes at first. Yamaha was originally Nippon Gakki. It made piano frames. But pianos weren't a promising industry. There wasn't enough wood to make more instruments. Nippon Gakki's president was worried. He thought the company wouldn't get enough business. In 1953, he told a group of employees to do something new. He told them to make a motorcycle engine.

Nippon Gakki began selling the YA-1 in 1955. The motorcycle's frame was dark red. It became known as the Red Dragonfly. It was stylish. And it performed well. Nippon Gakki's first motorcycle was a success. The motorcycle group became its own company. It was named Yamaha Motor. The piano company later changed its name to Yamaha Corporation.

FUN FACT
Yamaha Motor's logo features three musical tuning forks, just like Yamaha Corporation's logo does.

Yamaha soon started making dirt bikes. Most bikes in the 1960s weren't meant for off-road riding. The ones that were could be expensive. Yamaha changed that in 1968. It designed the DT-1. It was made to drive off-road. And it was affordable.

Yamaha provided bikes for a motocross star. His name was Bob "Hurricane" Hannah. He rode a Yamaha 125 0W27. Yamaha had worked hard on its suspension. Hannah raced in the 1976 National Motocross Championships.

The DT-1 was Yamaha's first off-road bike.

Bob Hannah was inducted into the Motorcycle Hall of Fame in 1999.

The first race didn't start out well. Marty Smith was in the lead for eight laps. Smith had won two championships. But then, Hannah made his move. He passed twenty-one other riders. On the next lap, he pushed his way past Smith. The fans were shocked. Smith couldn't catch up. Hannah won the race! He went on to win the championship. His Yamaha bike helped him do it.

Yamaha keeps improving its dirt bikes. It wants to give customers products that will improve their lives. Today's Yamaha dirt bikes do just that.

FUN FACT

Yamaha makes bikes for street riding, motocross, off-road riding, and more!

Yamaha dirt bikes have changed a lot since 1955.

CHAPTER 3

Track and Trail

Naoki is a motocross racer. He rides almost every day. He's an **amateur** racer. There's a big race coming up. He wants to do well. He hopes to compete professionally soon.

Naoki climbs onto his Yamaha YZ450F. The body is white. A streak of light blue accents the seat. The seat is made of stiff foam. It makes the bike more comfortable.

The dirt on the motocross track is deep and soft. But Naoki can handle anything. He can change the bike's map. This setting affects the bike's engine and handling. He uses the Power Tuner app on his phone. No other company has an app like this. It hooks up to the bike. Naoki can change his bike's settings. He sets his bike up for the track.

FUN FACT
Yamaha has a team for amateur racers. It's called the bLU cRU.

The YZ450F is made for motocross racing.

Naoki loves the bike's suspension. The 2019 model has a stiff suspension. Its **fork** has coil springs inside. The springs give a good balance. The bike absorbs shocks from bumps. And it's still easy to control. Naoki makes lap after lap on the track. He practices his skills over **whoops** and jumps. With his YZ450F, he'll go pro in no time.

Naoki's sister Ami also has a Yamaha. But hers is designed for cross-country racing. Her YZ250X has a two-stroke engine. The powerful bike carries her along mountain trails. She rumbles through grassy fields.

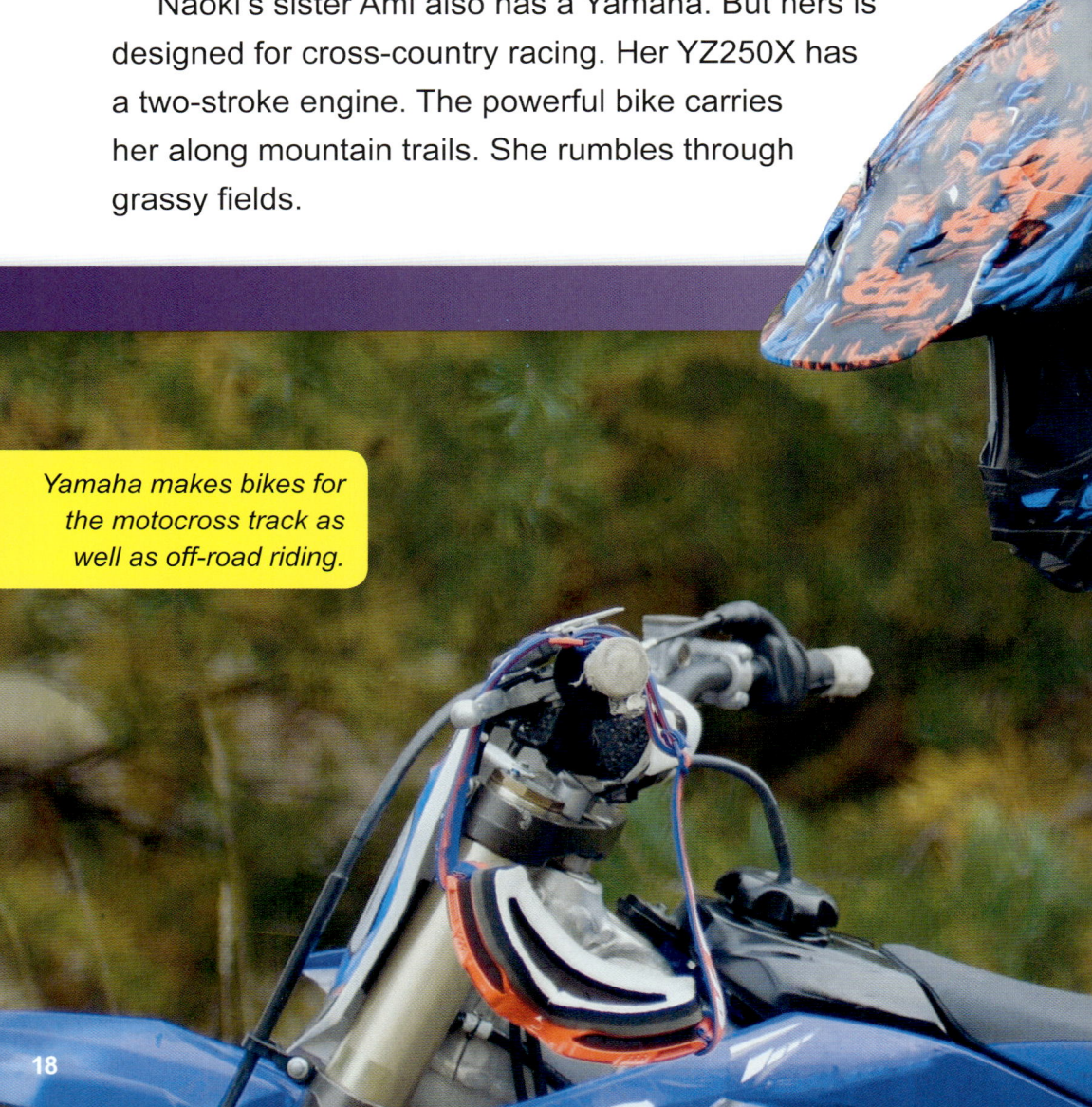

Yamaha makes bikes for the motocross track as well as off-road riding.

Ami competes in the Grand National Cross Country series. The races are long. She has to go much farther than a motocross racer. That's why the YZ250X has a bigger fuel tank.

The YZ250X has great suspension. It's made for off-road riding. The bike goes over logs and rocks. The suspension is softer. The tires are different, too. The tire walls are wider. This helps Ami drive over big rocks. She doesn't get a flat tire.

Ami and Naoki use dirt bikes for very different sports. But they both love their Yamahas. They're glad that Yamaha makes dirt bikes for anyone.

BIKE MODEL	YZ125	YZ450F	YZ250X
SUITABLE FOR	Motocross	Motocross	Cross-country
ENGINE SIZE	125cc	450cc	250cc
ENGINE TYPE	Two-stroke	Four-stroke	Two-stroke
TYPE OF START	Kick-starter	Electric	Kick-starter
BASE PRICE	$6,499	$9,299	$7,499

COMPARE AND CONTRAST
YAMAHA DIRT BIKES

YZ125

YZ450F

YZ250X

CHAPTER 4

Kiara Fontanesi was a gymnast when she was younger. But her brother rode dirt bikes, and she wanted to race, too.

Yamaha Champs

In Italy, a Yamaha racer has made history. Kiara Fontanesi is the most successful woman in motocross. She's won six Women's Motocross World Championships. That's more than any other woman. She started riding dirt bikes at age three. Her first bike was a Yamaha PW50. She entered her first World Championship in 2009. She was fifteen. She didn't win the championship. But she won the final race.

In 2012, Fontanesi won her first championship. She was way ahead of the other racers. Fontanesi won her sixth title in 2018. She rode a Yamaha YZ250F for each championship.

FUN FACT
Fontanesi won her first race when she was six years old.

Across the ocean, American Aaron Plessinger has become a Yamaha star. His dad was a cross-country champion. Plessinger liked riding in the woods. But he liked motocross more. He had an amazing year in 2018. He rode his YZ250F in both motocross and **supercross**. He won his regional 250cc supercross championship. Then the motocross season began.

Plessinger won his first motocross championship in 2018.

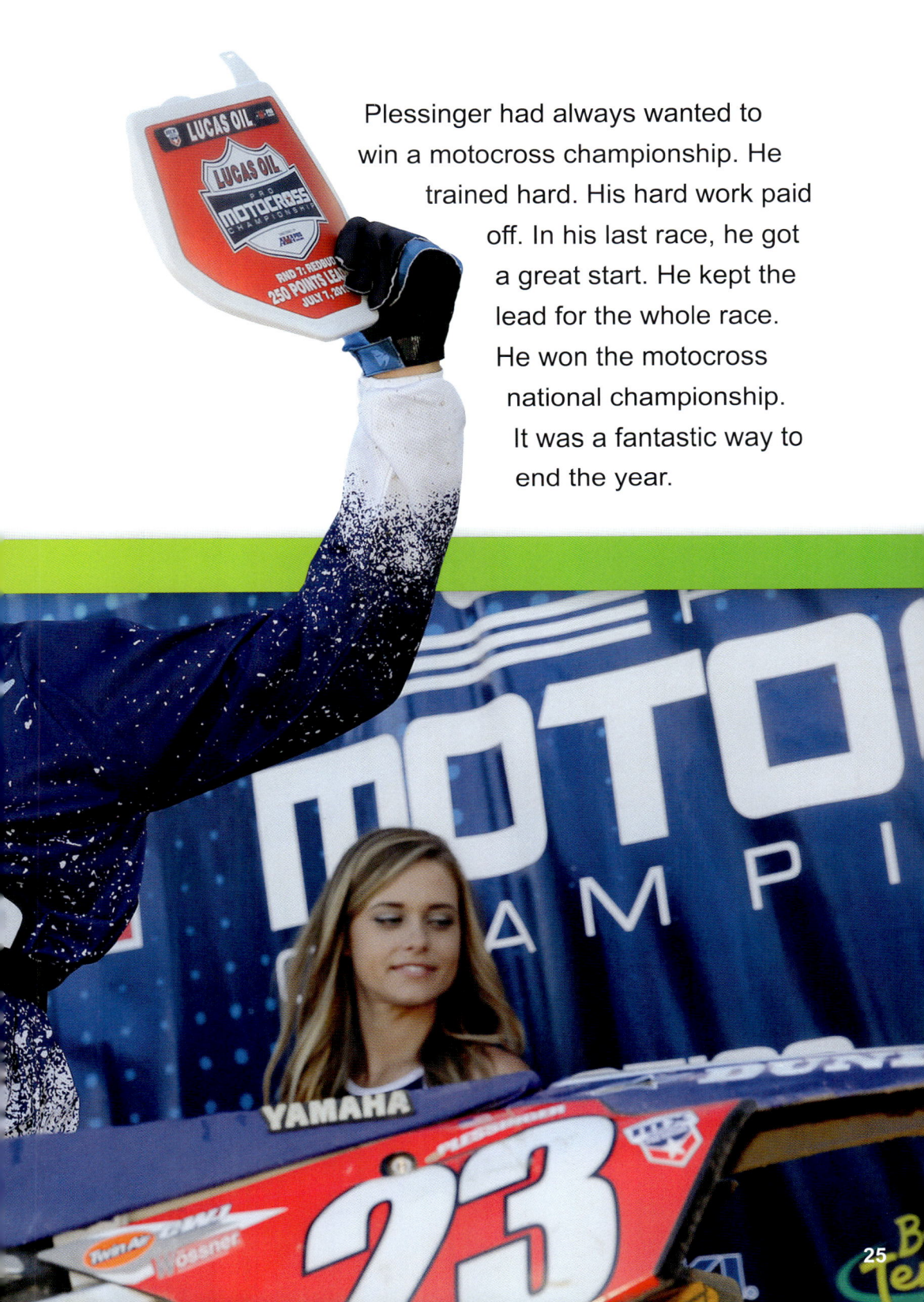

Plessinger had always wanted to win a motocross championship. He trained hard. His hard work paid off. In his last race, he got a great start. He kept the lead for the whole race. He won the motocross national championship. It was a fantastic way to end the year.

Yamaha is a great brand for all kinds of racers.

Yamaha helps all kinds of racers succeed. Amateurs and professionals win races on Yamaha bikes. There are bikes for trail riding, cross-country racing, and motocross. The bikes have changed a lot since the 1968 DT-1. Yamaha keeps raising the bar.

DIRTY BIKES, CLEAN WATER

Yamaha gives back. Some of its employees in Indonesia were struggling. They didn't have clean water. The company wanted to help. It designed the Yamaha Clean Water Supply System. It helps people in developing countries get clean water. The system is being installed around the world.

BEYOND
THE BOOK

After reading the book, it's time to think about what you learned. Try the following exercises to jumpstart your ideas.

THINK

THAT'S NEWS TO ME. Kiara Fontanesi has won six FIM Women's Motocross World Championships. This makes her the most successful woman in motocross. How might news sources be able to fill in more information on her 2018 championship? What new information could you find in news articles? Where could you go to find those news sources?

CREATE

SHARPEN YOUR RESEARCH SKILLS. The book mentions cross-country races like the Grand National Cross Country Series. Where could you go in the library to find more information about cross-country dirt bike races? Who could you talk to who might know more? Create a research plan. Write a paragraph about your next steps.

SHARE

WHAT'S YOUR OPINION? The text states that Yamaha has bikes for anyone. Do you agree or disagree with this position? Use evidence from the text to support your answer. Share your position and evidence with a friend. Does your friend agree with you?

GROW

DRAWING CONNECTIONS. Create a diagram that shows and explains connections between Yamaha dirt bikes and pianos. How does learning about pianos help you to better understand Yamaha dirt bikes?

RESEARCH NINJA

Visit **www.ninjaresearcher.com/0950** to learn how to take your research skills and book report writing to the next level!

RESEARCH

DIGITAL LITERACY TOOLS

SEARCH LIKE A PRO
Learn about how to use search engines to find useful websites.

FACT OR FAKE?
Discover how you can tell a trusted website from an untrustworthy resource.

TEXT DETECTIVE
Explore how to zero in on the information you need most.

SHOW YOUR WORK
Research responsibly—learn how to cite sources.

WRITE

GET TO THE POINT
Learn how to express your main ideas.

PLAN OF ATTACK
Learn prewriting exercises and create an outline.

DOWNLOADABLE REPORT FORMS

Further Resources

BOOKS

Adamson, Thomas K. *Motocross Racing*. Bellwether Media, 2016.

Murray, Julie. *Yamaha*. Abdo Publishing, 2018.

Shaffer, Lindsay. *Dirt Bikes*. Bellwether Media, 2019.

WEBSITES

Factsurfer.com gives you a safe, fun way to find more information.

1. Go to www.factsurfer.com.
2. Enter "Yamaha Dirt Bikes" into the search box and click 🔍.
3. Select your book cover to see a list of related websites.

Glossary

amateur: An amateur is someone who participates in a sport for fun, not money. Naoki is an amateur motocross racer, but he hopes to become a professional one day.

clutch: The clutch is the part of the dirt bike that lets the rider change gears. The YZ125 has an adjustable clutch lever so that riders can change gears more easily.

fork: The fork of a dirt bike is a piece that connects the front wheel to the handlebars and provides suspension. Yamaha dirt bikes have springs in the fork.

kick-starter: A kick-starter is a piece on a dirt bike engine that is pushed down in order to start the vehicle. Yamaha's YZ125 and YZ250X are both started with a kick-starter.

supercross: Supercross is a form of motocross that takes place on a track in an arena or stadium. Aaron Plessinger won a supercross championship in 2018.

suspension: A vehicle's suspension system keeps it steady over obstacles and absorbs shock. Yamaha's off-road and motocross bikes have different suspension settings.

throttle: The throttle controls how much fuel or power goes to the engine. The throttle of a dirt bike is on the right handlebar.

two-stroke: A two-stroke engine is a simpler and lighter engine than a four-stroke engine. Dirt bikes with two-stroke engines can often go faster than four-strokes.

whoops: Whoops are a series of small hills on a motocross or supercross track. The right suspension system helps racers perform better on the whoops.

Index

blue, 8, 16

Clean Water Supply System, 27

DT-1, 12, 26

Fontanesi, Kiara, 23

forks, 9, 18

Hannah, Bob, 12–14

kick-starters, 4, 9, 20

motocross, 5, 12–14, 16–19, 20, 23, 24–25, 26

Nippon Gakki, 11

off-road bikes, 12, 14, 18–20

pianos, 11

Plessinger, Aaron, 24–25

Power Tuner app, 16

supercross, 24

suspension, 8, 12, 18, 20

two-stroke engines, 5–6, 18, 20

YZ125, 4–8, 9, 20–21

YZ250F, 23, 24

YZ250X, 18–20, 21

YZ450F, 16–18, 20–21

PHOTO CREDITS

The images in this book are reproduced through the courtesy of: smileimage9/Shutterstock Images, front cover, pp. 7, 8, 26, 30; Diego Barbieri/Shutterstock Images, pp. 3, 14–15; Pavel L Photo and Video/Shutterstock Images, pp. 4–5; Rmikka/Shutterstock Images, p. 6; Mathis Wienand/Yamaha Motor Co./Getty Images Publicity/Getty Images, pp. 9, 21 (top), 21 (middle); Grzegorz Czapski/Shutterstock Images, p. 10; hilalabdullah/Shutterstock Images, p. 11; Pat Brollier/The Enthusiast Network/Getty Images, p. 12; Eric Schweikardt/Sports Illustrated/Set Number: X22201 TK1 R9 F11/Getty Images, p. 13; Mirco Lazzari/Getty Images Sport/Getty Images, p. 16; Mark Sims/Icon Sportswire/AP Images, p. 17; Studio 72/Shutterstock Images, pp. 18–19; Red Line Editorial, pp. 20–21; Good Guys Motorsports, p. 21 (bottom); Lionel Vadam/PHOTOPQR/L'est Republicain/MAXPPP/Newscom, p. 22; Fabio Averna/NurPhoto/Getty Images, pp. 22–23; Jeffrey Brown/Icon Sportswire/AP Images, pp. 24–25; Watcharapol Amprasert/Shutterstock Images, p. 27.

ABOUT THE AUTHOR

R. L. Van is a writer and editor from Minnesota. She loves books, animals, and crossword puzzles.